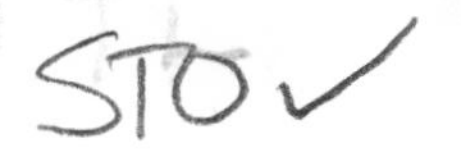

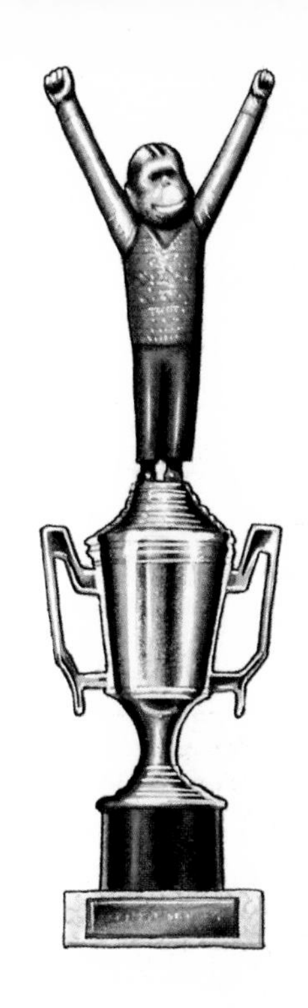

Anthony Browne

WILLY THE CHAMP

Alfred A. Knopf · New York

This is a Borzoi Book published by Alfred A. Knopf, Inc.

 Published in the United States by Alfred A. Knopf, Inc., New York, and simultaneously in Canada by Random House of Canada Limited, Toronto. Distributed by Random House, Inc., New York.
Originally published in Great Britain by Julia MacRae Books, a division of Franklin Watts, London.
First American Edition
Manufactured in Belgium

1 3 5 7 9 10 8 6 4 2

Library of Congress Cataloging in Publication Data
Browne, Anthony. Willy the champ.
Summary: Not very good at sports or fighting, mild-mannered Willy nevertheless proves he's the champ when the local bully shows up.
[1. Chimpanzees—Fiction. 2. Bullies—Fiction] I. Title.
PZ7.B81984Wf 1985 [E] 85-10053
ISBN 0-394-87907-4 ISBN 0-394-97907-9 (lib. bdg.)

For Ellen

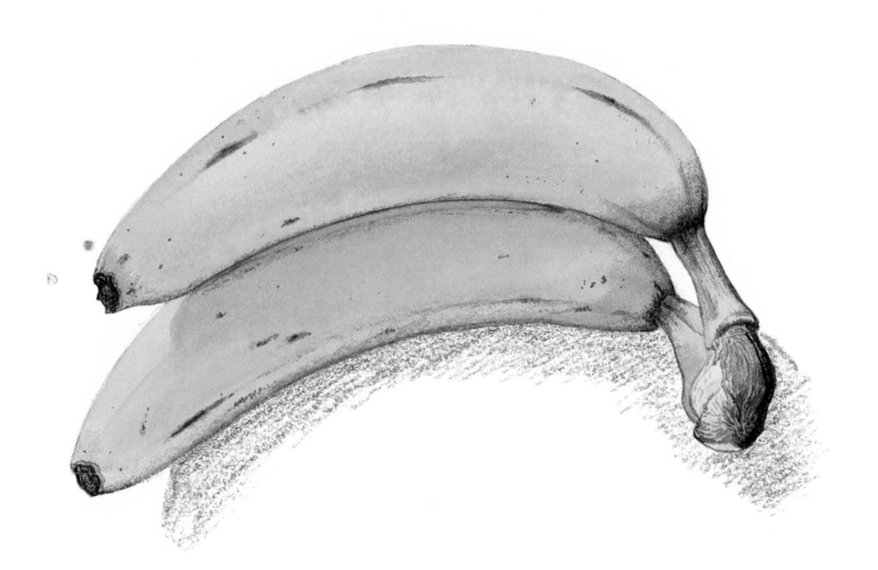

Willy didn't seem to be any good at anything.

He liked to read . . .

and listen to music . . .

and walk in the park with his friend Millie.

Willy wasn't any good at soccer . . . .

He did try.

Willy tried bike racing . . . .

He really did try.

Sometimes Willy walked to the pool.

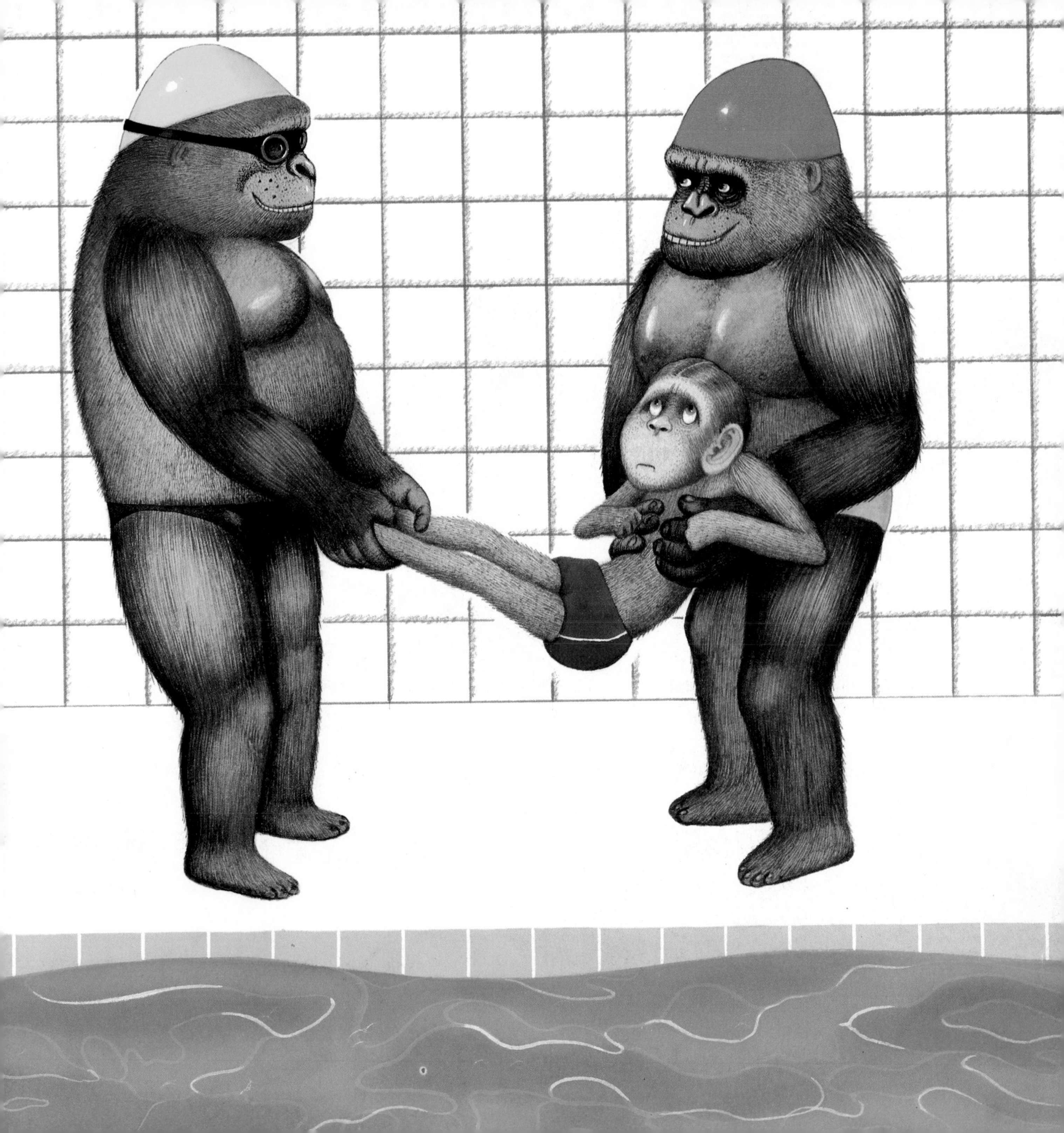

Other times he went to the movies with Millie.

But it was always the same. Nearly everyone laughed at him – no matter what he did.

One day Willy was standing on the corner with the boys when a horrible figure appeared.

It was Buster Nose.
And he *had* a horrible figure.
The boys fled.

Buster threw a vicious punch.

Willy ducked . . .

then he stood up!

"Oh, I'm sorry," said Willy. "Are you all right?"

Buster went home to his mom.

Willy was the Champ.